Seed School
Growing Up Amazing

Joan Holub

Illustrated by
Sakshi Mangal

SEA GRASS

Whoa!

I'm falling!

© 2018 Quarto Publishing Group USA Inc.
Text © 2018 Joan Holub
Illustrations © 2018 Sakshi Mangal

First Published in 2018 by Seagrass Press, an imprint of The Quarto Group.
6 Orchard Road, Suite 100, Lake Forest, CA 92630, USA.
T (949) 380-7510 F (949) 380-7575 www.QuartoKnows.com

Seagrass Press titles are also available at discount for retail, wholesale, promotional, and bulk purchase. For details, contact the Special Sales Manager by email at specialsales@quarto.com or by mail at The Quarto Group, Attn: Special Sales Manager, 401 Second Avenue North, Suite 310, Minneapolis, MN 55401 USA.

ISBN: 978-1-63322-374-5

MIX
Paper from responsible sources
FSC® C101537
www.fsc.org

Design: Nick Tiemersma
Editor: Barbara Ciletti

Printed in China
10 9 8 7 6 5 4 3 2 1

For you, an amazing kid. —JH

To all the children:
Never stop believing in your dreams. —SM

Whee!

Where am I going?

I think I'm lost.
Is this a garden?

"Welcome to Seed School! My name is Ms. Petal," the teacher tells the little lost seed.

The other students in the garden have questions.

Where did you come from?

Where did you get that spiffy hat?

What kind of seed are you?

I don't know.

Ms. Petal has questions, too, for the whole class. "How are you all alike?"

"We are seeds!" they say.

"How are you all different?" she asks.

"We are different sizes, shapes, and colors. Some of us are bumpy or smooth or wear shells. And we will grow up to be different plants!"

"What will I grow up to be?" asks the little lost seed in the spiffy hat.

"Patience," says Ms. Petal. "It's only fall. We have the entire season to learn about growing."

But the other seeds came from this garden. They all know what they will grow up to be.

THE LEGUMES KNOW.

I will be a bean vine.
I will grow my seeds in pods.

I will be a peanut plant.
My peanuts will grow
underground.

THE WEEDS KNOW.

I will be a dandelion
with yellow flowers.

I will be crabgrass and
spread out and hang on
tight wherever I grow.

FRUITS AND VEGETABLES KNOW.

I will become a vine that grows
the biggest fruit—pumpkins.

I will be a carrot. My orange
part will grow underground.

THE FLOWERS KNOW.

I will be a tall, happy sunflower.
My face will turn to watch
the sun move across the sky.

I will be a pretty daisy,
one of the most
popular flowers of all.

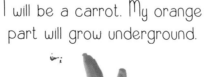

"I have a spiffy hat," says the lost seed.
"Maybe I will be a vine that grows hats."

There are four things we need to grow up:

SOIL

SUN

WATER

AIR

When we are planted, we will sleep in the soil. We'll wait for the sun to warm us and for the rain to get us wet. Then we'll push up out of the ground.

In P.E., we practice dirt diving.

We do push-ups so we will be strong enough to push our stems up through the soil when it is time to grow.

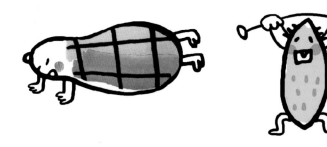

We learn the top two rules of growing:

STEMS UP
Stems carry minerals and water up to a plant's leaves.

ROOTS DOWN
Roots are like straws drinking minerals and water from the soil. They also anchor plants, so they don't fall over.

We sing the Growing Song to help us remember:
Grow, grow, grow yourself,
reaching for the sun.
With our roots in the soil to drink the rain—
growing up is fun.

"I like singing," says the little lost seed.
"Maybe I will grow up to be a music plant."

Rock-a-bye seed
hanging in the tree top
when the wind blows,
the seed will drop...

Mary had a little seed,
little seed, little seed...

Old MacDonald had a seed e-i-e-i-o.
And from that seed, he grew a plant.
e-i-e-i-o...

One day, the little lost seed asks, "Can we grow now? What are we waiting for?"

"For spring!" Ms. Petal replies. "It's my favorite season. What are your favorites, students?"

We like FALL.

We get to fall away from home and
go to school to learn how to grow.

We like WINTER.

We get to take a long, snuggly nap.

We like SPRING.

It's warm, which helps us
grow into plants and blossoms.

We like SUMMER.

We will grow some more,
and then we'll make new seeds.

On library day, we visit the Leaf Librarian.
She tells us about food and photosynthesis.

When you become a plant, your leaves will make
food for you using photosynthesis.

1. Rainwater flows up through your roots.

2. Your leaves take carbon dioxide from the air.

3. Green stuff in your leaves called chlorophyll
   traps the sun's energy.

4. The energy helps mix water and carbon
   dioxide into food. Dinner is served!

Leaves release
oxygen that people need
to live back into the air!

What did the plant say to the
hungry caterpillar?

Dunno. What?

Leaf me alone.
Haha!

"I am good at jokes," says the little lost seed.
"Maybe I will grow up to be a joke bush."

What did one flower say to the other?

You're my best bud.

What did the dirt in the garden say when it rained?

If this rain doesn't stop, my name will be mud!

The flower seeds read aloud a book report. "Most plants grow flowers that make seeds. Inside each seed is the hope of a new plant."

My daisy will last all spring and summer.

My sunflower will make 1,000 to 2,000 seeds!

My pumpkin flower will last one day.

Principal Bee buzzes busily by to tell us some nectar-ific news.

Hey, howzz you doin' seedzz?
I'm here to tell you about pollination,
so listen up.

I get nectar from
flowerzz, see?
Pollen sticks to me.
I tell you that stuff is annoying!
Luckily, it rubzz off on other
flowers I visit and helps
them make their seedzz.

When spring comes
I'm gonna be buzzy —
I mean busy.
Buzz you later. Bye!

Soon the weather turns chilly.
Fall is over. Winter is coming.
School's out. It's graduation time!

Ms. Petal hugs us and says, "Good job, seeds!
You are ready to move on now—to bring new
color and joy to the garden."

I'm not sure I'm ready
to graduate.
Can I stay with you?

And then we're off!

We spread out around the garden.
Some of us travel by squirrel tail or bird beak.

Others go whirling and twirling in the stream
or riding on our friend, the wind.

WE LAND.

We snuggle in wherever we are.

The wind blows a blanket of leaves
and dirt over us to keep us cozy.

We nap all winter
long, waiting.

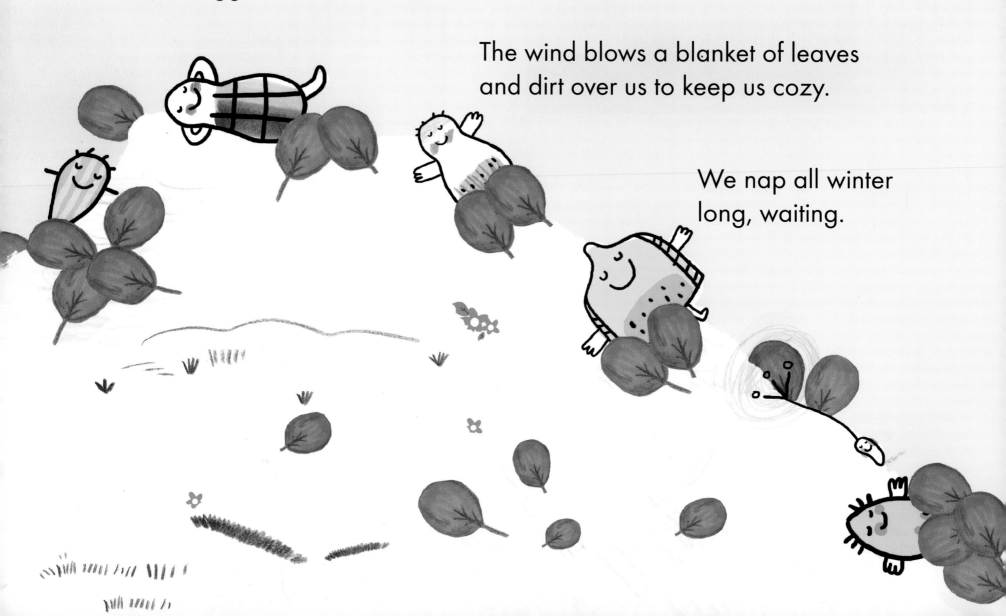

Then one day we wake up. It's warm. It's spring.

TIME TO GROW!

SEED SCHOOL GARDEN

THE SEEDS SPROUT INTO SEEDLINGS...

THEY GROW INTO PLANTS...

THAT ARE SPLENDID.

By the end of the summer, the garden is in full bloom.

Sniff, whimper...

But the little lost seed is still small. He still wonders what he'll become.

Fall comes again, then winter,
spring, and summer.

Years go by.

The little lost seed's
plant gets bigger,
and so do his hopes.

"I hope, I hope, I hope that I will grow up to be something amazing."

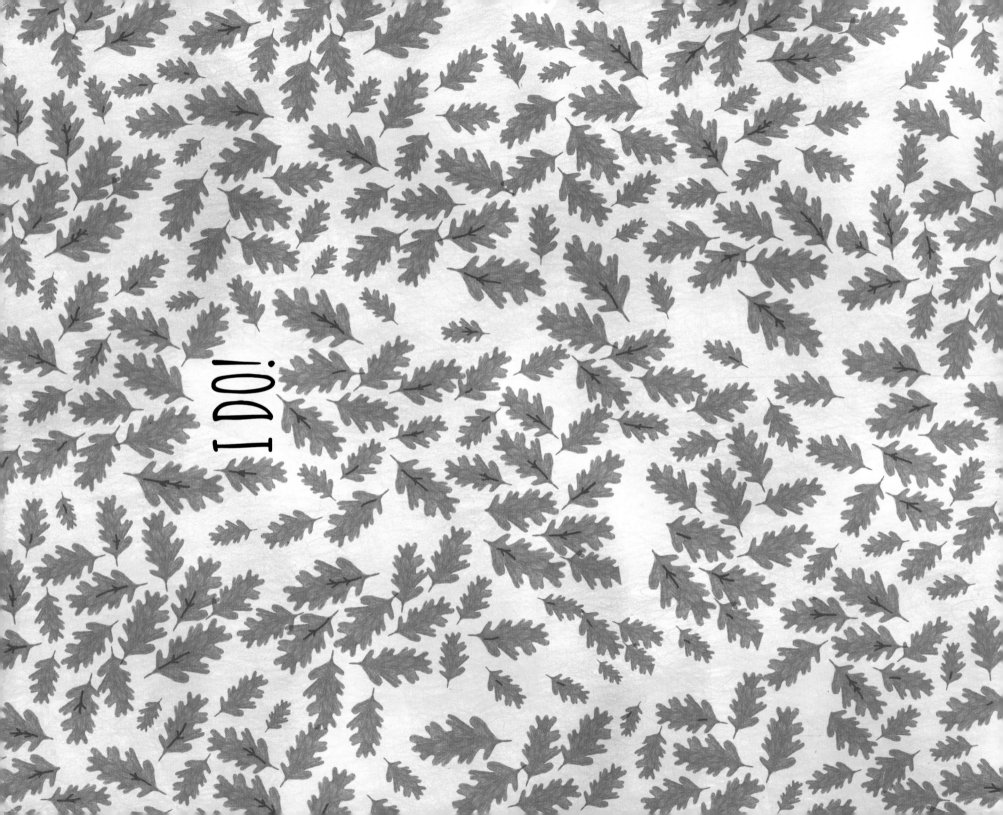

I DO!

A MIGHTY OAK TREE!

Turns out I was an acorn, a nut
with a seed inside. And look!
I grew more little acorns,
all filled with the hope of growing
up to be mighty oak trees . . .
just like me.